The Naughty Boxer

Story
John Prendota

Illustrations
Paul Hughes

There once was a boxer who liked to play. He would play all day if he had his way. He would play inside, he would play outdoors. He would play and play, but never get bored. Now my dog Roland is almost two, he misbehaves and likes to chew. He chews on this, he chews on that. Roland will chew and chew, shoe after hat.

His coat is that of tiger stripe, brown and black, the brindle type. Floppy ears and saggy lips, giant paws with cotton tips. There is no yard he can't destroy. He gets loud and rowdy with his squeaky toy. There's still one thing I must explain, it's his terrible gas that is such a pain. He lets them rip, I cannot lie. Like a ripened onion, they make mom cry. Now onto the adventure that is at hand, a story that goes from city to sand.

Today I awoke, a Saturday. The day every kid waits for to run and play. Roland and I side by side. From the warming sun we cannot hide. Running and jumping is how we glide. Off to the park, to the wonderful slide. Now only Roland would take this leap, a leap quite steep to the sand so deep. I run around to see if he's fine, with a shake of his fur he's back in line.

So I tell him "let's go boy," we have much to see. On the dark green grass he stops to pee. Embarrassed am I with kids all around, he lifts his leg and goes to town. The others laughed and so did I. He is quite a hoot that dog of mine. I'm a little relieved it's not number two, as I forgot the bag, the bag for poo. Oh my gosh it's almost one. We have to get home to have some lunch.

We made it home to take a break. Grilled cheese and milk, it tasted great. The ice cold milk and the gooey cheese are a perfect match that always please. Mom turned her back to grab some more, so I dropped a gift down to the floor. Mom never says yes it's always no, but I can't help it, I love him so. I always find a way to sneak, sneak to Roland a delicious treat.

Roland still has to eat his food. Unlike the grilled cheese there is no drool. I sometimes wonder why and why, he has to eat that food, that food so dry. What if he ate the food like us? What's the big deal? Why the fuss? Then I remember what mommy said, the food we eat would drop him dead. Always feed him what he needs, to grow up strong not to please. If you want the best for your loyal friend, this one rule you cannot bend.

After lunch we have no plans, in the yard kicking sand. So I ask my mom "what's to do?" She said "if you're bored you can clean your room." I reply "that's no fun on a Saturday!" I looked at Roland; his eyes said "play". Off again with our bellies full, to enjoy more time away from school. We head to Billy's house in a rush. He has a Boxer named Bella, Roland's crush. Her coat is that of fallen snow, a brown spotted eye if you must know.

Now he runs with happy feet, faster and faster down the street. I keep an eye as he runs ahead; "never too far" is what I said. He stops and waits for me to catch up, my loveable huggable boxer pup. The sky is blue without a cloud. The neighborhood is busy, people about. Tending to their perfect lawns, there's nothing like yard work to make me yawn. Why do grownups like that stuff? Week after week it's never enough. Cut the grass pull the weeds trim the hedges and plant the seeds.

Roland and I have other plans. The time for trouble is at hand. Things seem to go awry when we walk by. Garbage cans tipped over, circling flies. Roland rummages through the trash, yesterday's dinner, chicken and mash. I yell at him "Mr. Corncobbs get out of there! That food is so gross and full of hair." Roland is starting to get out of line. If no one sees us we'll be fine. Still far from Billy's, he is waiting for us. Too bad Roland can't ride the bus.

When we arrive it's almost four. Bella's big wet nose is against the door. Drool and boogers line the glass, of the large oak door, handle of brass. I ring the bell, Roland can't wait. To dance with Bella, his doggie date. The door swings open and he bullies in. The battle is on, but who will win? A tornado of paws, slobber and fur, they move so fast it's quite a blur.

Billy's mom is not impressed. Her face is drenched in worry and full of stress. Her eyes are fixed on the red vase she loves, the china cabinet and the antique rug. As they continue to wrestle about, she blows her top and begins to shout. "Get those two outside right this minute!" She grabs a bag of treats and reaches in it. With one tasty snack they're out the door. Staring intently, hoping for more.

We start a game of fetch, but did not see, an open gate, a chance to flee. Roland and Bella hit the jets. They rocket off right through the fence. "Let's go Bella! Let's go today, on a quick adventure, not run away. Back and forth up and down, we will see the city all around." Roland and Bella are in a tizzy. For the next few hours they'll be quite busy.

The first stop on this trip for two is the butcher shop, for things that moo. Tommy always has a snack for them, a juicy sausage or a slice of ham. At the back door they beg and plead. Roland and Bella refuse to leave. Tommy comes out with two large bones. As he makes them wait they whine and moan. Roland looks at Bella rather confused; with Tommy's teasing he is not amused. He finally gives them what they crave. That juicy bone, it makes their day.

Tommy finally has to say goodbye, impatient customers wait inside. These two scurry down the alley past a van, pawing each other with their boxer hands. Bella and Roland hit a puddle for a drink. Think of a mink and you have your stink. This dirty water is not from the tap. A mile a minute is how they lap. Water on lips make quite a slap. Slobbery tongues that go flibbity flap.

Suddenly a fuzzy fat squirrel darts past their feet, then two and three, a family. Once Roland and Bella catch their scent, the chase is on to the vent. This vent you see is a hole in the wall, large enough for a squirrel, but not a dog. They have only one chance, they make a dash. It's over in a flash with one big crash. All Roland gets from this race so close, is a bump on his head and a scratched up nose. This bump he has is two inches tall. A common result when head meets wall.

This happens to Roland P. Corncobbs all the time. His pride is hurt, but his health is fine. He yells to Bella "I've had enough, let's head to the place where the waters are rough!" Bella snickers, she's quite amused. He is always upset when his ego is bruised. With a smirk on her face Bella gives the nod. She leads the way like the Iditarod. To play on the beach is what they crave, bothering people and tackling waves. It takes some time to travel this far, crossing the streets and dodging the cars.

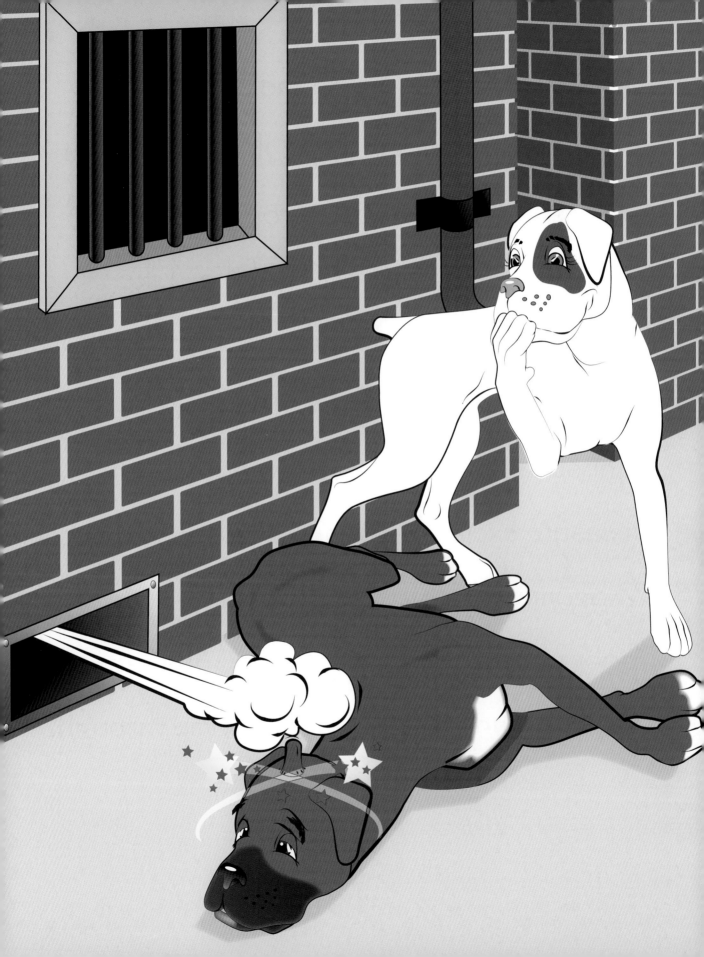

As they reach the pier it's a view from the top. Of a field of blue if blue was a crop. The sand is so white, so white it looks fake. Like in a movie or a picture you'd take. They take a minute to look over the crowd. It's Christmas day for these two hounds. To measure excitement it never fails, use the (wagometer) known as their tails. These poor people they have no clue, unaware of the hurricane that's about to come through.

With a hop and a leap they're down to the sand. Their first victim is an overweight man. A man with a body shaped like a pear. He has fear in his eyes as he continues to stare. Now Roland and Bella are quite harmless you see, but with no way of knowing he turns to flee. Large man in a Speedo with a hideous tan, Fanny pack, headphones and a bratwurst in hand. It doesn't take long to make up the ground, with a flick of her paw Bella knocks the man down.

Bratwurst and lotion fly all over the place. The man's sandal comes off, he falls on his face. Roland gobbles the brat as the man starts to shout. "You dogs are trouble! Who let you out?!" "Bella, I think it's time we should go." A crowd started to gather to check out the show. A last bite of sausage and Roland lets out a blast, a blast of gas that needed to pass. A fact was proven when he let out that fart. They ARE trouble you see, trouble at heart.

Not wanted around they head up the shore. Trouble is fun, they're looking for more. Always competing they want to see, who is faster and who will be? To be the fastest is important to them; it's instinct from birth, wanting to win. Bella is quick she takes the lead. She could be a sled dog no matter her breed. As fast as she is, Roland comes back. He takes the lead with his running attack.

Down to the wire it's neck and neck. A photo finish is what to expect. What a race! One that's too close to call. This will decide who is quicker once and for all. Right at the end Roland gives a last leap. Instead Bella's the winner, a victory she'll keep. Bella is laughing and giving him grief. He thinks she cheated she must be a thief. She stole that race; it was his fair and square, although in truth it's his loss to bear. It takes a big dog to admit a defeat, but Roland will never admit, admit he's been beat.

With the sunset splashing over the seashore rocks and the seagulls circling over the shoreline docks, these two signs tell Roland it's time to go. He has to get home to his blanket and bowl. While making their way off the beach, they spy a picnic basket just out of reach. The owners' busy, their heads are turned. Bella and Roland grab a snack, then turn and burn. Running and eating is not well advised, making their way past the incoming tides.

These food burglars head back up the hill. They want off of this sand, they've had they're fill.

After a day in the sun the sand is so hot. Their paws are aching, hooves they are not. Almost to the top, but Bella missteps, she tumbles back down and lands with a crack.

She tries to stand up and gives out a yelp. Her leg it is broken, now weak as kelp. It is getting dark, the beachgoers have all departed. Bella is starting to shiver, their condition uncharted.

Roland tries to help by licking her paw. They would be ok if someone saw. Except no one saw, they're all alone. He lies down by her to keep her warm. An hour has passed, it is pitch black now. "How are we going to get out of this? Oh how? Oh how? We're going to be fine Bella, you will see." It's beginning to storm, Roland spots a tree. He moves into action and grabs her scruff. "This might hurt a little, it will be quite rough."

Roland pulls and nudges to get her safe, from the lightning, thunder and crashing waves. Hunkered down they are very scared. To be home and warm is a wish they share. It is very late and they need some food. Instead they have growling stomachs and sinking moods. Most of this rain the tree cannot stop. Their fur more sopped with every drop. Bella jumps in fright from the sight of a light. Is it over she thinks, the end of the line?

In relief she sees a policeman approach. Gone are knots in her stomach and the lump in her throat. Roland knows this man, has seen him before. It's Officer Randy Bo Bandy, Say it once more! He is just an average cop, a hero to some. Randy IS a hero this day, their savior has come. Randy springs into action, a dog lover for life. He grabs a warm blanket and dials his wife. She's a veterinarian you see and a good one at that. She helps animals of all species, even the bat.

He lays her down gently in the backseat of his squad. Roland follows behind, never leaving his side. Randy flips on the siren and slams on the gas! Blowing through stoplights, every car he must pass! They all arrive without a minute to spare, rushed to the emergency room for urgent care. Roland paces and paces, the waiting cuts like a knife. He waits for news of Bella, the love of his life. The vet finally comes out, it felt like hours. The Dr. has done all she can, everything in her power.

Roland's so sad, but emotions change fast. Bella appears at the door with a limp and a cast. It's her! She's fine! It looks worse than it feels. The doctor says "six to eight weeks to fully be healed." Bella is drenched with kisses and licks. Roland would not give this up for a thousand sticks. It's been one heck of a day, had the time of their lives. A few bumps and bruises, but everyone's fine. Officer Randy Bo Bandy gives them jerky kept handy. With lips still sandy they gobble like candy.

A smile on his face, Randy picks up the phone. It's a long time coming, time to call home. He knows their owners, has met them before. On prior adventures galore Randy has knocked on their door. His first call is to Bella's and it rings and rings. Then he rings Roland's, after one ring a voice sings. His family is so happy, but with Bella's no luck. They will have a bath at Roland's house, they're covered in muck.

The bath is all done; they're clean as a whistle. With the dirt off his body, again he looks brindle. Bella also looks great, her coat as white as a sheet. On the end the bed is where they will sleep. Tomorrow she goes home, but now feels relaxed and toasty. Cuddled by Roland, tired, but cozy. Roland too is exhausted, his head next to hers. They dream of sizzling steaks and juggling bears.

I'm so glad they are safe, the last hours quite tense. From now on I'll be sure to lock up the fence. Roland P. Corncobbs is my BFF. If friendship was food, he'd be a wonderful chef. My dad comes in to wish me goodnight. With everything right he tucks me in tight. Mom told me today about your time at the park, with Roland claiming his territory and making his mark. You are responsible for him and the things he might do. So always remember your bag, your bag for poo.

The End

For my string bean
&
The Boxer, man's BFF

Printed in the U.S.A. by The Covington Group

ISBN 978-0-578-09227-0